THE HANDPRINT

THE
HANDPRINT

* * *

Lesann Berry

File No. 1
Alternate History Archive

ISINGLASS PRESS / SILVERLAKE

Isinglass Press
PO Box 1731
Castle Rock, WA 98611
www.isinglasspress.com

Publisher's Note: This is a work of fiction. Names, characters, places, and incidents are a product of the author's imagination. Locales and public names are sometimes used for atmospheric purposes. Any resemblance to actual people, living or dead, or to businesses, companies, events, institutions, or locales is completely coincidental.

Cover Design by www.NovelNeeds.com
Interior Design by www.BookDesignTemplates.com

Ordering Information: Special discounts are available on quantity purchases by corporations, associations, and others. For details, contact the publisher at the address above.

Silverlake / Lesann Berry — First Edition

ISBN 978-1-939316-17-2

Printed in the United States of America

Dedicated to Vincent Price.
Thanks for being the narrator in my head.

File No. 1, Alternate History Archive

The Alternate History Archive contains a collection of substantial stories sharing a particular universe, one in which historical events play out somewhat differently from the timeline we inhabit. Mostly. Written late at night and filed away inside the yellowed Egyptian linen folders of an antique wooden file cabinet, they collected dust and accumulated weight for a considerable period of time. One evening a bony finger poked my shoulder and suggested I share them. Thus, I submit File No. 1 for your perusal. So, please, pour a libation and enjoy.

~ L.B.

THE HANDPRINT

A Ghoulish Mystery

As a rule, Annabelle Lash tried to avoid close contact with law enforcement, especially since she left home. Once she took the nightshift job at the morgue, maintaining the practice proved more difficult. Tonight the uniforms were nervous. They hovered around her, closing ranks as they neared the porch. They all moved together, resembling a giant spider fueled by a cluster of dark-clad legs.

One of the officers peered down at her, checked her cleavage, then her ID tag, and tried to make conversation. "World's gone crazy, right? First, that business in Omaha and now here."

Uncertain how to respond, she hefted the heavy bag more securely on her shoulder, realized she should probably say something and opted for a safe question.

"What happened in Omaha?"

All eyes turned to her and she almost stumbled as she became the focus of scrutiny.

"Don't you watch the news?" another cop asked. His tone clearly indicated she couldn't be that out of touch with the rest of the world. His unibrow flattened into a single blonde slash as if to punctuate his disapproval.

"I'm new to town. Just moved in and haven't had time to get my internet or cable hooked up." Her stuttered explanation seemed to satisfy them.

The first cop jumped in again. "Some crazy bastard slaughtered a bunch of locals in a two-night killing spree in the Capital neighborhood. City personnel spent the last three days scraping up remnants."

"Wow," Annabelle said, unable to hide her shocked expression.

Her feet slowed. Stomach clenching with a sick dread, she swallowed the splash of acid bouncing up from her gut. She feared she knew all too well what the Omaha disaster was about.

Once they showed their credentials again and moved past the secure checkpoint, her momentum decreased even more. In an effort to widen the distance from the cops, she stopped and dropped her bag to the damp concrete. Rain had fallen all day but the night shone clear. Stars winked from a solid black sky. She took thirty seconds to unwrap the white disposable protective suit morgue staff were required to wear when working with body fluids.

From what she'd heard in the initial report, she needed to wrap up before she descended to the basement, the scene of the crime.

Her delaying tactics worked.

The uniforms flowed on without her, eager now to get away from public scrutiny. She stuffed the plastic wrapping in the pocket of her canvas field kit and tucked the Tyvek jumpsuit between her elbow and ribcage. The last one to climb the steps, she cast a quick glance at the herd of news reporters and camera crews standing on the sidewalk.

They were unusually quiet and subdued, but as soon as her gaze turned on them they shouted out questions.

"What does the Coroner's Office think is the cause of death?"

"How does this scene compare with the one across town last week?"

Douchebags. She hadn't even been inside yet. Ernie had repeatedly told her to ignore the media and repeat the standard mantra. So she did.

"I can't offer a comment at this time."

A line of yellow police tape stretched across the perimeter, restricting access for the mob of spectators which manifested at every macabre scene. This one was no different except the people wore silent grave faces. The city waited, breathless for details about the latest find but they also hesitated to hear the news.

Gruesome killings spooked the public.

The stench grew thick before she reached the open double doors.

The immaculate turn-of-the-century Craftsman architecture featured the typical tri-color paint job found up and down the streets of the Innsbruck Quarter. She'd never seen this part of town. Usually, she stayed at the office while senior technicians visited crime scenes. Tonight her luck meter had run dry. The unthinkable had struck in the heart of the safety zone, the fancy river-front estates where the richest of the rich put their stockinged feet up on the hearth.

The cop posted at the door stopped her by holding one hand up in front of her face.

"Coroner's Office." She lifted the ID tag hanging from her lanyard and tapped the plastic triangle against his palm, turning to show the black and white picture and raising her chin for comparison.

He waved her on. "Hope you brought a body suit, sweetheart."

"You know it, Officer Hearthrob." Ernie had also told her not to take any shit from the uniforms. Her boss insisted if she let them push her around, she'd regret stepping foot on a crime scene.

"Watch it, smartass." He said to her back but his words carried no bite.

She pushed through the entry into an elegant parlor. Along with the clean suit, the terse report they'd received at the office suggested they bring something to scoop up what was left, like a squeegee.

And people wondered why she didn't enjoy socializing with cops.

Annabelle clamped her free hand over her nose, but even with peppermint oil dabbed around her nostrils, the fetid odor seeped into her mouth. The tang of clotted blood was a familiar flavor she could ignore but the meaty effluence of perforated viscera flooded her palate with saliva.

She silently cursed the circumstances leaving her the solitary on-duty staff member tonight.

"Make way." A voice bellowed somewhere in front of her.

People jostled and the view ahead opened up to let a uniform stagger out of the crowd. He collapsed to his knees and vomited a watery gruel on the cream carpet at the edge of the living room. She joined the line of people stepping around the retching man as she approached the interior basement entrance. Her steps slowed as her tummy flipped again. Despite being the last one in, and the only female present, none of the officers teased her about lagging behind. Nobody even gave the uniform grief for up-chucking inside some rich guy's house. The scene must be a bad one.

She paused to assume the folded hazmat suit. Veteran investigators clustered to the left side, their pasty faces all featuring tight lips and flat eyes.

"Just like the others," one of them said to another.

The second man nodded and responded in a similar vein. "Yeah, same handprint but nothing printable on the rough surface."

"Bastard's going to slaughter his way across the city and back."

She knew about the string of attacks beneath other tidy clapboard homes. Few secrets missed the scrutiny of those who tended the dead. A given expectation of the job was what happened in the morgue stayed in the morgue. Once someone hit the autopsy table they shared most of their privileged information. Now that violent tragedy had struck one of the upper crust affluent neighborhoods, an extra measure of urgency layered atop all the others. Dead politicians and administrators upped the ante and demanded results. More heads were going to roll, at least figuratively, and the pressure steamrolled downhill flattening the working schmucks trying to catch the Handprint Killer. Herself included.

A grizzled officer climbed up the last stair and exited just as she reached the doorway. "Going down, lass?" he asked in a thick Irish brogue.

She nodded, somehow the accent made the endearment pleasant rather than offensive.

"Here's some free advice. Don't. If you still gotta go, take a deep breath and hold it until you come back up." He clapped a hand over her shoulder and squeezed as he broke and rushed past her, his face grey and green at the same time.

Annabelle zipped up the white billowy suit, let the hood hang down her back for now, and slung the bag across her shoulders in order to avoid tripping on anything. As advised, she sucked in air and began to descend. Each foot placed in the center of the painted wood planks, she moved with cautious precision, trying not to tear her flimsy white surgical booties on a jutting nail head. The shoe protection reminded her of a cheap Halloween costume. Underneath, even with the layer of insulated thermal silk underwear, her thin cotton scrubs felt insubstantial in the cold moist air.

She descended almost to the bottom before scanning the space.

An officer stepped aside and called out, "Make way for the Coroner's Office."

She appreciated the assistance but needed a minute to gain a sense of what was on the floor.

"Thanks, Officer," she said, just to be polite.

"I'll never get used to this kind of stuff."

She ignored the cop's mutter and looked around. From where she stood on the lowest step, light blazed.

Lamps mounted on raised industrial tripods lit the entire space, reaching into the corners in a vain attempt to beat back the shadows. The basement matched the footprint of the huge house and despite the number of lights, pockets of shadow survived. Sodium bulbs cast a bluish glow on alabaster complexions, the wash of illumination potent enough for a professional photo shoot. Up close the techs appeared as if they'd been dipped in bleach, their skin almost bone-like. The bright beams exposed every inch of stained concrete in the center of the space and drew her gaze. The illumination cast the scene into a harsh modern art expose. The victim's remains, a woman most likely based on the size of the single femur, lay in tattered scraps. The long bone evidenced spiraling green fractures where the assailant had cracked open the cavity to suck out the marrow.

Annabelle shivered.

Something unspeakable had taken place below the pristine oak floors of 2112 Larkspur Lane.

Hunger had fed.

The space smelled vile. Deep gauges gashed the floor. Dust comprised of Portland cement mixed with body fluids and formed a muddy pink paste. A pretty curvilinear design curled in the sludge.

Annabelle found the finger painting more unsettling than the carnage.

On the wall above the swirl was the perfect imprint of a human hand. In her mind she imagined someone bracing themselves in order to heave their gorged body up from the concrete floor.

"Haven't seen you before, I'd remember. You part of the nightshift crew from the morgue?"

The question came from her right hand side. She turned and found a slender man in a rumpled charcoal suit leaning casually against the stair rail. Despite the fact he was no more than a yard away and totally worth staring at, she hadn't noticed him. The death scene consumed her attention.

With an accompanying nod, she said, "I'm new. And tonight I *am* the crew."

His eyes wandered up and down her body but the shapeless white jumpsuit foiled his desire for more information. "Tough draw for a first-timer. Promises to be a long night." He slouched, his profile shadowed by the stairwell, his dark eyes black as shiny beetles under narrow brows.

She returned the favor, her slow perusal noticing the excellent fit of a tailored suit and the elegant shoes. His voice was cultured, smooth as aged brandy. Sexy. She knew the type and liked the package, enjoyed the sound even more.

Stop that, she told herself but she decided he might be cute.

He tapped his chest. "Name's Detective Smithson. You are?"

Annabelle mumbled her response and tried to focus on doing her job but her gaze drifted back to the man. She found him staring at her.

"What?"

He shrugged. "You look pretty fresh for working the nightshift at the Coroner's Office, especially for being *the* crew."

Her lips curled into a sneer. "Doesn't say much for your powers of observation, super sleuth."

He grinned at her tart response.

The sight sucked all the moisture out of her mouth. *Hot*, her mind sputtered. *Very hot.*

She whistled in a deep breath and forced her thoughts back to work. She looked at the scene, mentally assessing the most efficient method for collecting the tissue remnants...

Her brain balked.

A frigging rake and shovel offered the best bet, but since her equipment and supplies lacked both tools, she'd need to improvise. The royal blue body sack tucked inside the standard issue field kit she checked off as equally useless. A hefty bag would work better, size-wise. Hell, a Ziplock or two could probably do it.

Her first solo assignment sucked on ten different levels.

To worsen matters, she'd missed her midnight lunch break because she'd gotten called out here. The scent of death made her stomach growl. Another noisy rumble like that one and anybody might put dead parts and pale girl together and make ghoul.

"Peppermint?"

She turned her attention back to the sexy detective. Smithson stared at her intently for a moment and then his hand darted out. She glanced down and found a red and white tin in his palm.

Well, well. Small world.

Snagging the package she popped the lid and selected three of the pungent smooth disks, slipping them under her tongue. Better. The fumes masked the tantalizing smell and immediately softened the cramps.

"Thanks, appreciate the offer." She returned the breath mints and slid her gaze across his, decided he was in fact, devastatingly close to smoking hot.

"Oh god, you're going to make me puke. How can you..." The officer standing next to them charged up the stairs, his hand wrapped over the lower half of his face.

Smithson winked at her, his gaze dropping to watch as she worked the peppermints around her mouth. A tiny frown formed on his forehead and his eyes narrowed.

Recognizing his intense interest, she tamped down her own intrigue. Biting off the smile threatening to curve her lips, she turned away. "Gotta get to work now, Sherlock."

"I'll be around all night, Sugar."

His voice followed her but she didn't find his use of the endearment disparaging. *Harlot*, she accused herself and snickered.

Clearing the scene was messy long work. Thank god the morgue stocked hazmat suits in the van or she'd be wearing a considerable portion of the deceased. Working between the crime investigation techs, they dodged around each other, trying to avoid collisions as they all attempted to complete their tasks.

One of them paused to ask her, his mouth twisted into a parody of a smile, "You going to use the wet/dry vac to get the rest?"

"Not a bad idea," she admitted and wondered if she should check with her boss and see if they had one in the supply room.

The blood spatter tech backed up a step. "Whoa, and I thought *we* got desensitized on the job." He shook his head and retreated.

Smithson wheezed out a sneaky laugh near her ear. "I like your style Annabelle. Very practical."

She swiveled and met him nose-to-nose. His warm breath tickled her lips. "Why are you still here?"

"Detecting." He wiggled his golden-brown eyebrows.

"Detect anything interesting?" She almost cringed at the breathy quality in her voice.

His dark eyes burned into hers. "Oh, yes. I expect to conduct a follow-up investigation later tonight. Several critical questions require answers and I can't wait."

The blatant interest fluttered her pulse and then flustered her. She pulled her eyes away and studied the room. Nobody paid any attention to them. Bright lights lit the garish handprint on the wall and she said the first thing that popped in her head.

"Wasn't a similar print found at several other scenes?"

When Smithson didn't say anything she looked back at him. He studied her with speculative regard.

She shrugged. "I heard one of the detectives mention it upstairs."

He nodded. "Can't tell if the doer is the same perp – the clarity is good but the surface never allows the techs to pull the actual palm or finger prints – but the similarity is still hard to ignore."

A voice from the other side of the room called him away and Annabelle returned to cleaning.

Hours later she carried her gear back outside through the gauntlet of uniforms. Security measures had been relaxed. As the mess was removed the gravity of the situation abated and the twisted humor resurfaced.

Her stomach growled. She was starving.

Smithson jogged up beside her as she crossed the lawn.

"Finished up?"

She nodded. "How many does this make?"

He seemed to understand she wanted to know about the killings. "Over the last year we've had a new victim turn up on average of one a month. But they aren't evenly spaced. It's not as if the killer works on some sort of schedule. At least not one we've figured out. The gap has been as long as twelve weeks between kills and as little as four days."

"I grasp the difficulty of discerning a pattern." She transferred the trash bag holding her soiled hazmat suit under her arm and surveyed him through a fringe of eyelashes. "Guess that's why they call you a detective, eh?"

He whistled an appreciative tune. "You aren't like the typical morgue attendant."

She gave him full-on attention. "You think? Your deductive skills are impressive. You must base your conclusions on the fact I speak in full sentences."

His laughter tugged something deep in her belly.

"I like you Annabelle. You're fun." He pulled one of the straps from the heavy canvas satchel off her shoulder and helped carry the weight. "To be honest, I think we've missed a lot of other victims. We've compiled a growing tally of nameless people, the kind nobody notices right away when they disappear. Appears to fill in some of the gaps."

She darted a quick glance at him as they walked up to her county issued van. "You think there're more?"

He nodded.

They stopped at the rear of the vehicle and she dug in her pocket for the keys. Even the media had departed the scene. She bet all the neighbors had locked their doors and climbed into bed, struggling to fall asleep with the hall light on.

"So, Annabelle." Smithson lingered over the pronunciation of her name, a smile curving his lips as he enjoyed her shiver of reaction.

He made her old-fashioned moniker, the one she'd always disliked, sound sensual and exotic. The tremor of awareness pulsing inside her burst into a flare of desire.

"If you're going to hide in plain sight like the rest of us, you need to take extra precautions around the force." He jerked a thumb over his shoulder. "Guys like this make the job harder for all of us. Controlling your appetite is the first step to successful assimilation. Here –"

He handed her a business card.

Bemused, she read the words printed on the front and back. "You're shitting me. Detective, are you telling me we have our own twelve-step program?"

His riff of laughter carried an undertone of appreciation. "Not quite. It's an early warning system, a telephone tree of sorts. You scent any sign of an out-of-control feeder, you call the number on the card. We'll send in a team to head off discovery."

Annabelle motioned toward the house with her chin. "What went wrong today?"

An odd expression crossed Smithson's features. He swung open the rear doors and sidled out of the way, helping her lift the bag. She shoved it under the crash cart.

"He fell off the wagon, again."

She leaned inside and deposited the folded-over nylon sack containing the victim on top of the gurney. She debated over buckling the straps and decided against.

She peered back over her shoulder, caught him admiring her ass and aimed a half-hearted kick at him. He hopped sideways. "He? You *know* who's doing this? Who are you talking about?"

Smithson leveled a gaze at her, raised his eyebrows in a way indicating he expected her to understand.

"What do you mean?" she demanded, turning around.

He sighed. "Nobody said anything to you?" Seeing her blank expression, he continued, "Your boss, Annabelle. Every so often he goes on a bender."

She shot him a dirty glower. "You're telling me Ernie Baxter, the Coroner, did this?"

He nodded.

"For real?" She slumped back to perch her butt on the bumper and crossed her arms. "Well hell, somebody on graveyard shift could have told the new ghoul."

"They never do," he said with a grin, his eyes dipping down to glance at her chest. Leaning forward he rested a palm on either side of her, his face only inches from hers. "So, since you're fresh off the turnip truck, why don't you let me treat you to dinner? I'll show you where to find the best roach coaches around town. You'll know how to grab a snack no matter whether it's day or night," he jerked his head back at the house and its hidden crime scene, "and next time you won't be caught off-guard."

Smithson had surpassed smoking hot and ventured into the realm of heretofore unknown desirable quantity. He smelled warm and delicious, ready and willing to satisfy an entirely different sort of appetite. Admitting she was hungry for both him and food, she capitulated.

"Okay, G-man, let's eat. You buy but then I fly. Apparently I've got to get back and fill out a ton of paperwork so my boss, who it turns out, is the perp – that's what you called him, right? – can sign off on the forms in the morning. This is so screwed up." She scrubbed a hand across her forehead.

Smithson leaned in even closer and sniffed her hair. "You're so hot you sizzle, Annabelle. I prefer a little spice in a woman."

Annabelle dragged the heavy crash cart with practiced hands. She had the process refined to an art. Unlike the first weeks she'd tried to guide the bulky carts silently down the halls, lurching drunkenly between the walls, now she let the gurney bounce off the interior corridors, clattering as she careened toward the autopsy theater. She plowed into the swinging door, the frame scraping against the bare metal hinge of the doorframe, the screech making the two other morgue employees cringe.

"Christ almighty, Annabelle, did you miss anything coming down the hall?" Jimmy stuck a finger in his ear and stirred.

Michael kept his hands slapped over the sides of his head. "For someone so small, how do you make so much noise?"

She grinned at them, her iPod tuning out the incessant bitching and complaining.

"Suck it up, peons. I'm the night crew manager, remember?"

The title meant nothing important, other than her ass was held accountable for anything bad going down. Still, she relished wielding power over the rest of the staff.

Just like her mother?

She shuddered. Now there was a thought ugly enough to twist her head around backwards. Ignoring her fellow employees, she hummed along with the song in her ears.

Ernie had said, "I'm going to have to put you in charge, Annabelle. You're the only one capable of stringing three words together while walking in a straight line."

True enough but she considered the promotion an accomplishment. Hell, before she'd come west and been employed by the Coroner's Office she'd never even had a real job.

"Just try to stay away from the cameras and reporters," Ernie cautioned. "They always make us look bad."

No problem. She was happy to avoid public notice.

Six months into her creampuff position she'd learned some hard truths about living on her own. The first eye-opener was discovering she worked twelve hour shifts exposed to a smorgasbord she couldn't sample at her leisure.

"Help yourself to all the organ meats you want," Ernie said. "Families never ask for those after an autopsy. Cremations are a big bonus. You can add your name to the list for choice parts – you come up on the rotation, you get first pick."

The second dose of reality concerned how much time she spent mooning over a certain sexy detective with player written up and down, sideways and across every one of his perfect abs.

"Something about you just resonates with me, Sugar. I don't know what but you're special, Annabelle." He'd whispered the words in her ear the first night, licking down the side of her neck.

She'd melted into a puddle. Those same lame compliments stole her breath and made her knees go wobbly. *Every. Single. Time.* She admitted though, Smithson was persistent even if he was a slick bastard. Maybe he was worth just a little hassle.

"We have to stop meeting like this," he told her at the last crime scene, his wicked smirk already promising plans for them later.

And that was the third slap upside Annabelle's head: the County Coroner's little problem. Ernie was a man with a major appetite unfazed by normal dietary suppressants. The hidden minority of ghouls in the greater metropolitan area struggled to contain the wreckage left in the wake of Ernie's frequent feeding rampages.

She patted the plastic sheet affectionately. "Kinda sorry to see you go, Boss man."

Ernie had made her life hell every time he got snacky. More often than not, Annabelle was the one left cleaning up the crumbs. And inevitably, because they both worked the night shift, Smithson showed up and her self-control hit the floor along with her thong.

Her immediate supervisor being dead was going to impact shenanigans with her sexy detective.

He'll just have to work his charm a bit harder, she decided.

Inside the dissection room she slammed the gurney against the institutional green wall and gestured with both hands.

"Voila."

"Who's the stiff?" Jimmy asked, following her through the swinging door.

Annabelle waited until Michael turned to face her. "Our very own Handprint Killer."

"No way! Ernie's dead?" Jimmy dropped the organ bucket with a clang and trotted across the room.

Michael shifted nervously, torn between wanting a closer view and keeping his distance from the man who'd terrorized most of the staff.

Jimmy threw off the plastic sheet and grimaced. "Dang, get a load of that! Criminy, what happened to him?"

"Ernie's pretty much a Swiss-cheese kind of mess," Annabelle admitted, giving a dismissive flick of her fingers. "Guess karma kicked him in the head a few extra times. Somebody tried to eat the asshole."

Michael's eyes popped innocent wide. "Literally?"

She offered him side-eye with an accompanying sneer and ignored his question.

Jimmy flopped the cover back over the corpse. "Who could stomach so much of the tough old bastard?"

The door swung open and the trio swiveled to face the newcomer.

"I'm here to find out," Detective Smithson said.

His gaze locked on Annabelle and the way his brows inched together she knew he was already trying to figure out how to maneuver her into the nearest bed. And all the while he'd be continuing his full-court press to get her to spend more time doing team stuff. Couples sorts of things. Like going to movies and stopping into cafes for lattes and chatter, visiting museums and art galleries, even suggesting they go so far as to hold hands and walk the park. All of which terrified her no little bit. The entire shebang stank of commitment.

Detective Ross Smithson had definitely wiggled under her skin.

"Like an infected sliver," she said aloud.

He grinned at her as if he knew exactly what she meant.

"Missed you back on-scene, Sugar. You whisked the body away before the crime tech people even had a chance to photograph anything."

"Duh, bloodhound, that was the idea."

He smiled at her, the sensuous curve of his mouth accompanied by a lengthy perusal up her denim-clad legs to the white t-shirt peeking out the front of her untied blue smock.

Annabelle tried to ignore the shiver of heat uncurling in her stomach but found the act near impossible. Nipples hardening, every nerve ending in her body stood up and cheered.

"So who finally did Ernie in?"

Smithson shrugged at Jimmy.

"Has anybody offered to do a resurrection?" Michael asked.

Everyone turned amused faces toward the morgue attendant.

"You offering?" Smithson wanted to know.

Michael backed up, his head shaking, mouth opened in a long denial.

"Don't anybody do it on my account," Annabelle announced. "Although I'll kinda miss him, I'm okay with him staying dead."

Smithson eyed her, his lips twisting into a jaundiced grimace. "Who's the next in line for being in charge of this place?"

"Mrs. Cox, the front office manager. At least until they hire a replacement –"

The partially digested corpse reared up on the gurney.

Annabelle stumbled back. The plastic sheet dropped away and a garbled moan burbled out from between Ernie's crooked lips.

Michael keened out a high-pitched wail.

Jimmy skittered backwards on his heels until he hit the wall.

Smithson casually reached into his jacket pocket and pulled out a small rectangle made of black plastic. The Taser resembled a television remote with a gun handle. He pointed the device and calmly electro-shocked the Coroner.

Jimmy recovered the power of speech. "Dude, that's rad!"

Michael huddled beside his coworker, eyes rounded into zeroes.

Annabelle studied the steaming body. "Ernie's a zombie now, isn't he?"

"Appears so." Smithson winked at her. "As if I don't already have enough paperwork to fill out before we sign off on this evening's fun." He shoved the door open with one shoulder. "Officer Griggs, these young men need to give a statement. They just witnessed the suspect rise from the dead."

Michael and Jimmy scrambled out at a full sprint.

Smithson turned back and met her gaze. "You never call."

She rolled her eyes. "Don't start blame-shifting." She jabbed a finger at her boss. "Is he getting up again?"

Smithson slipped off his coat and slung the garment over a piece of equipment. "We should drop him in the incinerator soon. The second jolt seldom works as effectively."

He grabbed one end of the gurney.

She yanked on the other and steered them through the maze of autopsy tables. "I land all the weirdos," she muttered.

"You want to catch something to eat after shift?"

Annabelle ignored him. Since her last lapse in judgment at the conclusion of a late night death scene almost a week ago, she no longer trusted her willpower. She'd tumbled into a clinch with the man and damn near humped on the rear fender of his car in full view of god and everybody. Thankfully everyone else had already left or they'd never live down the event. She'd been dodging his calls all week.

They slid her former boss into the crematorium chute feet first, flames licking out from twin rows of tiny gas jets. Before she could swing the door shut, Smithson backed her up against a wall.

He trapped her legs between his and kissed her neck. "Annabelle, why do I get the impression you're avoiding me?"

She shuddered as heat coursed through her body. Hands splaying flat on the institutional paint, she concentrated on trying to keep from clutching at his waist. "Might have something to do with the fact I never call you back?"

Ross raised his eyes and pierced her with a hard stare. "Be straight with me, are you seeing someone else?"

She shot him an offended scowl and poked him in the gut with her index fingers.

"Explain how I have the opportunity to meet anyone, Ross. If I'm not scraping up dead folks for my murderous boss, I'm pulling double-shifts because the morgue can't employ anybody – besides me – with an IQ over seventy. Not to mention the rest of the time I'm trying to keep my panties from hitting the deck when you come round – which, by the way – is pretty much at least once a week, sometimes twice."

"I wish it was more often, like nightly."

She finished speaking, breathless from the spate of words, as Ross's lips hovered only millimeters from hers. He'd just pressed his mouth to hers when Ernie climbed out and dropped to the floor.

They turned to look and he gave them a thumbs-up.

Annabelle frowned and pushed at Ross's shoulder.

He bent his head and planted a quick hard kiss on her lips. "I'm not complaining about our extra-curricular meet-ups but just once I want to wine and dine you like a proper beau, Annabelle."

"He's making a nice offer," Ernie said, clearing his throat and pointing at her. "Detective Smithson treats you good, you shouldn't dismiss his attentions."

Annabelle glowered.

"Stop helping," Ross told Ernie. "I thought you were a zombie now?"

"Think I must be immune." Ernie sneezed and yellow scum flowed out his nose.

Annabelle grabbed the fire extinguisher off the wall and swung the tank at Ernie's head. At the same moment, she heard Jimmy yell out in the hallway. Michael's high-pitched scream cut off midway. The red canister bludgeoned her former boss across the forehead.

Ernie's skull bounced off the asphalt tile floor and he blinked startled eyes up at her. "What was that for, Annabelle?"

"Take a gander in the mirror, you ass. For god's sakes, Ernie, you're sporting a full load of zombie juice. Go gargle or something before you poison everyone."

Pandemonium reigned inside the morgue. Shouts came from the lobby. Crashing noises echoed down the corridors. The sounds of chairs and file cabinets being tossed against walls clattered. Shattered glass popped and crackled like champagne corks.

Smithson ran for the source of the commotion, pulling his gun as he charged toward the melee.

Annabelle dropped the fire extinguisher and trailed Smithson out of the crematorium annex across the cold storage room and out into the dissection theater. When she reached the door his arm clamped around her waist and swung her back into the corner, pressing her tight to his side. He shushed her.

Her boss staggered in and gave her a pained expression. "Christ Annabelle, you should have been a professional thug." Ernie rubbed his temple, wiped his sleeve across his nose, stared at the yellow streaks and shrugged. Realizing his other arm was on fire he slapped at the smoldering remnant. He made a sad face at them. "I hate to think about relationship trouble between you two."

"Shut up, Ernie," Annabelle snapped.

Smithson turned and motioned for both of them to be quiet.

"And why'd you let a zombie chew off half your ass?" she asked in a stage whisper. She grabbed a baggie of red sloppy bits from the closest autopsy table and tossed them at him. "Take the edge off, Boss. You've got a lot of regenerating to do."

Smithson moved them away and pushed the door closed. The metal panel contained no mechanism to lock in position since it swung from both directions. "Ernie, you are into some sick kicks, my man. Guess the world takes all types, right?"

Annabelle ogled Ross with a half-smile curving her mouth. "Fine, let's have a fancy dinner at an expensive restaurant sometime."

"Do you mean like a real date?" He grinned back at her.

She nodded, his obvious pleasure charming her despite her attempt to ignore him. Trouble was he did that more and more, chipping away at her cold aloofness.

Ernie upended the baggie and neatly swallowed half the contents. "The zombie caught me by surprise. I never seen one reanimate so life-like."

Annabelle half-turned toward him. "Exactly how animated was he?"

Ernie flushed. "Enough to consider a little slap and tickle."

"Oh, gross. You may want to make the whole world go round, but zombies Ernie, really?" She tossed the receptacle for organ tissues and headed for the cold room door. "Time for us to hide gentlemen. Kick your butts into high gear."

"What are you so gunshy about all of a sudden? Annabelle?" Smithson ran into her back when she stopped dead in the doorway.

She froze in mid-step, listened, turned and sniffed the air.

Ross stepped aside to give her more room and just watched her.

Ernie shuffled forward, the empty bag crumpled between his fingers.

"Crap. Too late," she said.

Behind them a body crashed into the frosted window. The tempered safety glass shattered into a spray of sparkling gems. Officer Griggs draped over the frame. His throat gaped, torn wide. His viscera spilled over the sill, a streaming coil of bloody intestine spewing out a green fountain of digestive juices. The sudden silence was marred only by the drip of body fluids from the man's ruptured torso.

The Coroner took a jerky step forward and licked his lips, eyes rapt on the carnage.

"Fight it, man. Not now!" Smithson clutched for Annabelle's hand.

"Ernie's losing control again," she said.

He was already hungry, craving sustenance to aid his recovery from the injuries he'd sustained. No way was he going to withstand the alluring scent. He had so little self-control to begin with. Two simultaneous things happened. The outer door crashed open to show a zombie framed in the antiseptic light and Ernie lost the battle with his internal hunger.

The animated corpse shambled forward, the patter of rapid feet echoing.

Ernie threw himself at the steaming gore.

They collided in midair.

Unprepared for the rabid masticating of Ernie's jaws, the undead went down in a tangle of limbs, sliding in Officer Griggs' offal. The struggling forms slapped hard into the wall.

One glance at the zombie and Annabelle recognized his pinched features. She panicked. Both hands wrapped around her detective's arm, she dragged him back into the refrigerated room. Once inside she closed and latched the door. They were trapped in the dead-end wing of the morgue. No emergency exits or loading docks funneled inventory in and out from this end of the complex. They stood little chance of survival unless they could barricade themselves inside somehow.

Even Ernie's insatiable hunger couldn't match this challenge, surely? Besides, she knew this particular zombie was motivated. He was clearly still pissed at her.

Smithson frantically pushed buttons on his cell and shouted into the speaker.

Annabelle listened, trying to figure out what was happening in the next room. Meaty slaps and wet cries carried through the wall. Sooner or later one of them was going to burst the steel door wide open. Either way, things would probably end badly for her and Smithson.

The realization galvanized her into action.

They had corpses. She'd willingly sacrifice Mr. Paulson's cancer-ridden body if he slowed down the winner of the melee. Next gurney in line was Trilby Wilcox, a three-decade hooker. Annabelle doubted Trilby minded if a guy took a nibble or two. Rumor suggested she'd had pretty broad limits.

"Do you have a concrete plan for survival?"

Smithson snapped his phone shut. "Don't panic, Annabelle. I've called the cavalry."

A full-body thud against the door pulled them into a united front, hands clasped, fingers locked together.

The ponderous thump jarred Annabelle's confidence. Her hand tightened reflexively.

Detective Smithson turned in her direction.

She knew he was about to say something smarmy, one of those cheesy lines like men spouted in stodgy films from the nineteen-fifties. He might be hot enough to land her in bed on a regular basis but the man offered endless complications. Six months in her adopted city provided many intense new experiences to punctuate the point. Being trapped in the morgue halfway through the nightshift should qualify as a bizarre anomaly, but in truth, the event was too much a part of her life normalcy.

Oh God, she'd used the word normalcy.

Smithson grabbed her by the shoulders and shook until her head wobbled back and forth. "Dammit Annabelle, I'm baring my heart here and you're not even listening!"

She snickered.

He shoved her away, sent her stumbling into the corner just as the heavy door burst wide. The smidgen of guilt she'd been suffering about whacking her boss over the skull with a fire extinguisher evaporated.

Ernie clung to the doorframe. His eyes bulged. His mouth gaped. Blood and gore and various body fluids covered his front, his arms reddened and viscous to the elbow.

"Shouldn't the feeding frenzy be over?" she squeaked.

She scurried behind the last remaining gurney and motioned for Ross to follow her. The petite frame of the elderly woman beneath the plastic sheet didn't offer much distraction to a hunger-crazed ghoul in the grip of a frenzied attack, but Annabelle figured a snack was better than nothing.

Especially if the old maid delayed Ernie's strong teeth sinking into her own arm or leg.

She crouched down and peeked over Ms. Benson's flat bosom.

Poised halfway along the wall, Smithson's gaze remained on the room they'd recently vacated. Whatever he saw behind Ernie's bulk caused his mouth to go slack and his eyes widen.

"Ross? What do you see? What's out there?" Her voice sounded like a canary chirping.

Ernie swung his blocky head, expression vacant, and made vague pushing motions toward the incinerator room.

She winced. He might be telling them to retreat to the last remaining hiding place or he could still be pissed about the fact they'd tried to burn him up a few minutes ago.

"Move!" Smithson barked.

He followed the order with action, darting between the gurneys, scooping her up and scooting them through the old door. Inside the crematorium, the metal latch clanked shut behind them. They had nowhere else to go.

"If we put the fire out, we could crawl into the burn chamber."

Ross considered the narrow channel for half a second. "Not happening, Sugar. If something breaks down the big door the little one isn't going to help us much."

Silence filled her ears. Fluorescent lights humming overhead seemed loud. Ross said nothing but gathered her close and sank to the floor, pulling her down with him. Nestling her into his frame, he cradled her between his legs. Planting a kiss on her temple, he tucked her tighter to his chest and braced his back against the door.

Fear plucked at Annabelle. She lived with death on a daily basis, consumed death at every meal, dreamed over and even fantasized about death. The general public might spurn dying as something to be avoided, but for ghouls, well their existence revolved around the idea. They celebrated the end of life but she didn't want to die tonight and until now she'd never been frightened of the concept.

Her stomach growled.

Smithson's forehead dropped on the back of her neck. A shiver of breath warmed her shoulder blade. "Only you could be hungry at a time like this, Annabelle."

"It's not midnight, I haven't eaten lunch yet." She snuggled into his lean chest. "Who's Ernie about to meet?"

"I requested the cavalry. They sent a cleaning crew."

She twisted her head to catch the soft words. His cadence slowed as scuffling sounds filtered in from the neighboring room. A bellow made her jump. Ernie?

The lever rattled.

Smithson's arms tightened convulsively around her. His body stiffened as he pushed back, scrabbling his feet for purchase and fighting to put pressure on the door.

A grunt of sound was followed by a cacophonous howl of bleats and snarls.

Annabelle dug her rubber-soled shoes into the asbestos tile floor and pushed her weight against Smithson. She sputtered but questions eventually flooded out.

"Are you insane? You called in the fire brigade?"

Smithson laughed in her ear. "Annabelle you have no tact whatsoever. The fire brigade, I swear." He sounded genuinely amused. "Fire-breathers make the perfect clean-up crew. They burn everything to ash. All we have to do is a little sweeping up afterwards."

"Think they'll fry Ernie?"

"Probably. Especially if he tries to eat one, which he might. Don't get me wrong, I like the Coroner. But both our lives would be simpler if the guy didn't leave a regular trail of crime scenes littered with half-eaten bodies. Eventually, somebody's going to catch on."

Annabelle bounced forward an inch as a blow bucked against the panel. She ground her hips back into Smithson, grinned at his noise of discomfort and kept pushing.

"You're really turning me on," he grunted out between breaths.

A single slap, the flat of a hand striking a steel surface echoed in the small space. After a few seconds the silence resumed. The moment stretched out. Minutes passed.

Smithson nuzzled her neck until she squirmed on the cold floor. "I think this officially qualifies as bad timing, Detective."

"There's never a good time with you, Annabelle. I take what I can get. Especially if I may not live long enough to act out the fantasy I had planned for later this evening."

"You aren't getting anything tonight if we don't – " She broke off and sniffed experimentally. "Do you smell something?"

Smithson mimicked her action and nodded. Reluctantly he untangled their arms. "BBQ?"

Annabelle snorted and climbed to her feet. "I've been a bad influence on you, Ross."

His hand trailed down her side and squeezed the curve of her ass as they cracked the door an inch and peeked out. Ms. Benson still lay under her protective covering, ever the prim spinster. The gurney closest to the entrance supporting the body of Mr. Paulson, the improvised barrier Annabelle used to slow down potential pursuers, now contained nothing but a pile of black ash.

Smithson wove his fingers through hers as they inched into the room.

A garish red handprint decorated the outside. The familiar visual matched the many crime scenes. Ernie slumped against the wall next to his signature mark. His grey hair stuck up on end. A vicious burn blackened the left side of his face. His breath whistled.

His eyes focused on Annabelle and his lips twitched into a crooked grin. "This night shift business is hell," he said, the words rolling out of his mouth, hard as pebbles. "You need a raise."

"I'd high five you but I don't want the rest of your fingers to fall off. You look like hell, Ernie."

Ross grabbed a towel and scrubbed the telltale mark off the door.

Smoke curled from the hooker's overdosed corpse. She lay partly incinerated, the right half of her body compressed to formless dust.

Annabelle coughed into her fist, an attempt to cover an inappropriate burst of amusement.

Smithson grimaced. "Your sense of humor takes some getting used to, Sugar."

Ernie chuckled too, his massive chest quivering with suppressed pain. "C'mon, Detective Smithson, Trilby probably appreciated a fiery orgy. She'd have loved being the last victim of a smoldering assassination."

Annabelle rubbernecked but didn't spot another body. "I suppose the Zombie King managed to survive?"

Ernie nodded. "Fire crew took him into custody. Gonna be hard to keep him in lock-up though."

Balanced on one foot, she pushed the organ bucket over within reach and Ernie snatched up the contents.

Ross glanced at her, a sudden piercing expression sharpening his features. "How'd you know his identity? Why ask about him, Annabelle? You *guessed* the Zombie King traveled all the way out here from Nebraska?"

Ernie frowned up at her. "Aren't you from Omaha, Annabelle?"

She ignored their questions and sniffed the air. "Any idea why he was here?"

Ernie and the detective both stared at her.

"What?" she demanded.

"Spill it," Smithson said. "Don't leave out a single detail." The hard expression on his face suggested he wasn't playing.

She shrugged. "He got the wrong impression. Not my fault if a guy can't accept rejection."

Smithson speared his fingers through his hair. "Are you saying the King of the Zombies has the hots for *my* girl?" He sounded outraged.

Ernie laughed. "You're going to have to up your game, Detective Smithson. Competing with royalty is a notch above your pay grade, isn't it?"

"I can hold my own," Ross responded in a terse voice.

Annabelle grimaced. "I assure you it's unrequited. I never dropped trou for the guy."

Smithson grinned at her admission. "So, this guy's such a douche you actually left town to avoid him?"

"Don't get a case of the Galahads, Ross. I can handle Mickey."

"Mickey? The Zombie King is named Mickey?" Ernie dissolved into laughter, his battered body slumping further down the wall.

"I thought you were just a simple country girl," Ross said, accusation rising in his voice.

She gave him a blank stare. "Omaha happens to be surrounded by acres of countryside."

He planted his hands on his waist and glared at her. "I've been trying to lock you down for months and now I don't even know who you are."

Ernie's face lit up and he coughed out a watery crow of laughter. "Holy hell, you're the First Daughter!"

Annabelle shot him a glare that cut off his amusement with a sputter.

"You're the First Daughter?"

Detective Smithson's voice rose to a shout. He gaped at her like she was a complete stranger, his gaze sweeping up and down the body he knew practically as well as his own.

"The. First. Daughter." He repeated the words in a gloomy tone.

She waved her hands at him in a dismissive motion. "Let me tell you, the fame is way over-rated, Ross."

He pressed his fists to both sides of his head. "And to think I had a balls-out knock down fight with my mother over you and how you weren't good enough for her little prince."

Annabelle stopped and scrutinized him. "You did?"

His cheeks went red.

What a darling! "If we live through this you're so getting lucky tonight."

Ernie rolled his eyes. "You should've told me, Annabelle. It's risky having someone like you on staff –"

"Shut it, Ernie. I've cleaned up too many of your murder scenes for you to give me any grief about keeping secrets."

Ross grabbed her arm and spun her around to face him. "You could have mentioned it to *me*."

She snorted out a laugh. "You and I don't exactly spend our time talking."

He shook until her head flopped back and forth. "We might if you ever answered your damn phone, Annabelle."

She laughed, a slightly hysterical sound.

Ross eyed her suspiciously. "So if Mickey, the Zombie King, isn't a problem, why did you move all the way out to the coast?"

She sniffed again and the hair on the nape of her neck stiffened.

A figure moved into the doorway. Soft words slithered into the room and brought an answering silence. "Good grief. Look at this mess. Stop this nonsense at once, Annabelle. It's time you came home."

"Hello mother," Annabelle said with grim resignation.

"How dreadful your clothing is, and this place is just so, distasteful." The First Lady flicked her fingers at the body fluids dripping down the wall. "Whatever are you doing in this awful frontier town?"

Annabelle rolled her eyes. This was ground they had covered ad nauseum. "Avoiding a marriage disaster of monumental proportions, Mother."

"Don't try to be clever with me. Leave everything. Go outside. A car is waiting at the curb. You have considerable damage to undo and new alliances to create." She stared down her imperious nose.

Annabelle discovered she had no intention of obeying. "Stop mother. Just stop. I refuse to go back to Omaha. You can plot and scheme all you want but I'm not playing politics." She held up her hands in a placating gesture. "Ally the zombies and ghouls together by divorcing dad and marrying Mickey yourself."

She paused and leveraged an eye at Ernie.

He winked back.

"On second thought, you probably want to re-examine whether or not the two of you are exactly compatible. In truth, he might prefer dad."

The First Lady's severe expression turned thoughtful. "That explains a few things." She shook her head. "Nevermind. You're the heir apparent. This escapade is done. You must come home and manage your duties."

Smithson sputtered, swinging his attention between the women.

Annabelle's features hardened. "Why don't you just decide to live forever? Then you no longer need me. I get to have my own life. By the way," she yanked the detective forward, shoving him front and center before her mother, "this is Ross Smithson, heir apparent to the Smithson Manufacturing fortune. His family owns most of the state. He declared himself to me not twenty minutes ago."

Smithson kicked at her shin.

"Well, you did," she reminded him, dodging to one side and avoiding the blow.

The First Lady turned her attention to him. "I presume you're Senator Smithson's son?"

"Yes, Madame." He stiffened, spine ramrod straight, features sorted into a polite expression. His eyes stayed locked to her mother's gaze but Annabelle could feel him tracking her movement.

Ernie's eyes went round as he stared at the detective as though seeing him for the first time. "You're related to Senator Smithson? I thought the name similarity was a big joke."

Ross didn't even twitch but he flipped Ernie off, hiding his hand behind his back.

Annabelle took a step closer. "You see, mother? Everything's okay. I'm having a glorious rebellious stage, working as one of the regular folk so I can better connect with the common people, and I'm scoping out new political alliances like a good daughter."

She kneed him in the thigh when he opened his mouth.

Ross glared at her, eyebrows slashing the air as he tried to communicate something without speaking.

Her mother looked around, her gaze returning to rest on the two of them, standing side-by-side. A calculating expression filled her eyes and she pursed her lips. She studied Smithson for a long moment.

"As I recall, your mother is European?"

He nodded, sliding a glance over at Annabelle and preparing to jerk away from a well-aimed kick.

"Very good," the First Lady said and smiled at him, a pleasant cat-got-the-cream expression of satisfaction.

Annabelle's eyes narrowed.

"Well then, I'll let you get to cleaning up this little mess." She checked her label pin, a tiny glimmering gold watch. "I'll take care of things with Mickey, dear. Your father and I are at the Four Seasons. I'll expect you for dinner tomorrow evening. Eight o'clock. Do not be late." Her gaze flicked back to Smithson. "We dress formal, Mr. Smithson."

"Yes, Madame."

The First Lady turned and sailed from the room. The silence left in her wake reverberated with a dozen unanswered questions.

"Did you just receive an invite to dine with the First Family?" Ernie asked.

Smithson nodded. "I believe so." He turned to Annabelle for confirmation.

She pursed her lips. "I hope you're ready for the roller coaster ride of your life, lover. You just ousted the Zombie King and took first place at the top of my mother's matrimonial match-making list."

He grinned. "Guess you wish you'd called me back instead of forcing me to track you down again."

"Kiss me before I change my mind."

Smithson obliged and swept her into a tight embrace. "You could've just trusted me, Annabelle. I am a cop, remember?"

"What makes you think I don't trust you?" she asked, her lips pressed against his.

"Oh, I'd guess the first thing was the evasive answers, then the outright lies, and maybe the fabricated personal history – should I keep going?" Amusement flickered around his mouth. He pushed her gently away, leaning down to help Ernie climb to his feet.

"You have really sexy lips," she commented in a conversational tone as she rummaged for more scraps to tide Ernie over.

"Don't try to distract me." Smithson stalked around one end of a gurney, his gaze locked on her, wearing a serious face. "You really thought I wouldn't check you out?"

She laughed at his frustration. "Find anything?"

"Zilch." He studied her, his lips scrunching together. "And now I know why."

She handed Ernie another plastic baggie and waved at him. "Hey Boss, I'm taking the rest of the night off."

Ernie followed them out the door, grumbling. "I'll just take care of the clean-up, then."

"Did you slip something in my drink?" Annabelle blinked at the sunshine drifting across the floor of her studio apartment.

"I was going to ask you the same thing." Smithson wrapped his arms around her waist and jerked her back under the covers.

"If you don't let me up to pee, I'll make a mess."

"Charming." But his voice sounded amused. "My watch says it's only noon."

"Good work, Detective. You've explained why it's so sunny outside."

Annabelle padded over to the bathroom and pulled the door shut behind her. She turned on the faucet, not wanting him to hear her piddle. Not that any body function bothered Ross Smithson in the least. The son of a senator probably didn't have a self-conscious bone in his skeleton.

Unlike her. She snorted out a laugh. The pot just called the kettle black. But she left the water running.

A finger tapped on the panel. "Do you mind trading places?"

She grabbed her toothbrush and wandered into the tiny kitchen to rinse. A minute later he joined her, the spare one she'd left on the counter stuck in his mouth.

"You really going through with dinner tonight?" she asked. She washed off toothpaste residue and balanced the red stick on the edge of the sink. A senator's son probably had a fresh tuxedo hanging in his closet. Just in case.

"I am delighted to escort you anywhere, day or night." He rinsed too and set his next to hers.

They stood naked in the kitchen staring at their toothbrushes side-by-side.

"Chillingly domestic," he said.

"Yes, we are."

"Can I make a confession, Annabelle?"

"Sure." She didn't even peek at him.

"I've been crazy about you from the beginning. If I thought I could trap you into an arrangement, I'd jump at the chance."

"...but?"

He caught her chin and forced her to look at him. "My parents tried to dictate every life choice for me. They still attempt to make the occasional decision. I've always hated the interference." His smile turned down at the corners a bit. "I'd never try to do the same to you, no matter how desperately I want you."

She closed her eyes and smiled, her shoulders relaxing.

"And right there, despite my best efforts, is the reason I fell in love with you." She looped her hands around his neck. "You aren't really surprised, Ross. You can't tell me you didn't suspect."

"Well, I am a cop. We're suspicious that way." He leaned down and nuzzled her throat, squeezing so tight her breath whooshed out. "I hoped, Annabelle. I wanted you to love me but you're a tough read."

She sucked in a gasp and asked, "Aren't you going to say anything back?"

"Say what?" He blocked her knee with his thigh and twisted sideways. "Of course I love you, you blasted woman." He scooped her up and carried her across the tiny apartment, dumping her back into bed and flopping down beside her. "Allow me to demonstrate just one of the many ways I plan to love you from now on."

From somewhere in the crumpled pile of clothing on the floor, a ringing noise sounded.

"If you answer the phone I'll break your fingers," Annabelle threatened.

His lips feathered along her jaw. "Wouldn't dream of it, princess."

She stretched under his touch. "I'm not a princess."

"Not yet," he agreed, sucking at her collarbone.

His words filtered through the haze of her endorphin rush and she paused, slapping at his chest. "What does that mean?"

"What does what mean?" But he snickered in her ear. "You aren't the only one with an alternate identity, Sugar."

She groaned. "Oh god, my mother was a little too pleased about your mother being European. She knows something I don't, doesn't she? Where's your mom from?" She nipped his shoulder, leaving a red mark.

"Some tiny country beside an ocean. Nothing for you to worry over, I promise. Compared to the populous your family oversees, we're snack-size." Amusement dripped from his voice.

"Why does the phrase 'liar, liar pants on fire' come to mind?"

He grinned and pulled her tighter beneath him. "Because, unlike the typical morgue employee, you're capable of reasoning out basic logic. Your elevated IQ is quite a turn-on, in case you didn't realize."

"You're such a silver-tongued devil. You know what – your voice hooked me in the first place, you knew that already, right?"

Ross made a sound of agreement and yanked the covers over them both.

"I believe we're going to have a lot of fun together, Detective Smithson."

ABOUT LESANN BERRY

Crossing genre lines and leaping logic gaps, Lesann wiggles her literary fingers into as many fictional pies as possible – including contemporary and historical mystery, romance, speculative fiction, and even a little horror. Now she's mining the Alternate History Archive for the type of story she best loved back in the day.

Visit WWW.LESANNBERRY.COM for new releases.